THE ARRANGEMENT

Vol. 10

H.M. Ward

www.SexyAwesomeBooks.com

Laree Bailey Press

COPYRIGHT

Laree Bailey Press
First Edition: Sept 2013

THE ARRANGEMENT

Vol. 10

CHAPTER 1

There are many levels to the depths of Sean Ferro's anger, but holy shit, I never expected this. The man just stands there, on the sidewalk, and stares. It's like a nuke went off inside his head. Sean's big blue eyes don't blink, as his jaw becomes tighter and tighter.

Tipping my head to the side, I try to catch his eye. Nothing. Leaning forward, I poke him. "Uh, Sean? Not to be a diva, but I'm the one who should be freaking out right now, not you." And I am. I refuse to think about it right now, which is the only reason why I'm still calm. Denial is the best drug around.

That wakes him up. The muscles in his thick neck are strained like cords of rope. "Of course. I'm being unreasonable. Completely. This doesn't bother me at all. I mean, why should it? Why would I be upset if the woman I love is having three-ways with her roommate, sleeping with that dick Henry, and doing her best friend—who said he was gay until rather recently? It shouldn't matter at all. Of course not." Sean lets out a rush of air and presses his palms to his face and looks up at the sky as if thinking, *why me?*

"You tied me up and pretended to have a gangbang." I glare at him with my hands on my hips.

Sean peeks out from between his fingers and laughs. "Holy fuck, Avery." He starts laughing those light little laughs that sound more crazed than anything else. "I've never met my match. Not with business or in the bedroom, but you—we're neck and neck on the crazy scale, aren't we?"

I wave him off and grin. "Psh, you own the crazy scale, Sean. The Urban Dictionary entry for nucking futs is a picture of you." Folding my arms against my chest, I stare at the cracks in the sidewalk. How is it that this guy seems so right for me? We're both deranged lunatics. I'm pretty sure I'm committable and I know he is. I flick my gaze up and catch him staring at me. "What?"

Sean's trying not to smile. His lips keep twitching as his eyes dart between my gaze and the grass. "Nothing." He lets out a sigh and all the tension leaks from his muscles. Sean steps toward me, but he doesn't touch. The tension between us is thick. My body responds to him and remembers his caresses. "Tell me how someone pretended to be me last night. I'm guessing you were blindfolded or something."

I make a face and look away, wishing I could hide behind that bush down the street again. Being stupid is one thing. Admitting it later is another. Why is everything always crystal clear in hindsight? Avoiding his gaze, I say, "Uh, something like that. Listen, I can handle that on my own. Don't worry about it."

"No, you don't understand. It's *my* problem when someone impersonates me, especially if he took advantage of you."

"I'm a hooker, Sean. I don't think things work like that anymore." But I thought they did. I feel played, but the guy paid, so does it matter who it was? I honestly don't want to start turning over stones to see who did it, because I know I won't like what I find. Every day with Black becomes worse than the day before. I need a new job, but I'm so close to graduation. The end is within sight. I just have to hold out a little longer. I'm almost done.

Sean doesn't like that answer. I can see it in the set of his shoulders before he answers. "Avery, people will treat you the way you expect them to. This is unacceptable. What were you doing that you couldn't—"

Mel choses that moment to emerge from the house. "That is one fine house, Ferro. At least you're not a total asshole, cuz anyone who does stuff like this for his brother can't be all bad." Mel looks at me and then Sean. "What'd I miss?"

"Someone impersonated me to get to Avery."

My hands slam onto my hips and I glare at him. "Wow, thanks Sean. What if I wasn't going to tell her that?"

Sean's voice deepens as he glares at me. "If you say, '*You're not the boss of me*,' I'm going to throw you over my shoulder and spank you senseless." The look on Sean's face is dark and brooding. I know he means it. My response is so totally wrong, but a giggle pops out, so I press my hands over my mouth and look away, horrified.

Mel rolls her eyes and turns from us. "You two are into the freaky shit, and I don't wanna hear it."

Sean steps directly in front of me and looks down. "Avery is staying with me for a few days."

"No, I'm not!"

"Yes, you are. It's not negotiable."

Slouching, I tip my head to the side and counter. "Sean, you're being a dick."

"I am a dick." He lowers his face to mine, so we're nose to nose. "And it doesn't matter what you say, Avery, I'm not letting you out of my sight."

"Black won't let me stay with you."

"Black doesn't have to know." Sean glances at Mel and adds, "Does she?"

Mel makes an offended noise in the back of her throat and bristles. "Why you gotta be like that? I'm not tattling on you two if you want to fornicate, but Black does have eyes everywhere. In a couple of hours she'll know where we are and what we're wearing. She'll know Sean's here."

I glance up at him. Part of me wants him around. I want things to go forward, but this isn't forward. It's like a barn dance and I think we're spinning in circles, forever stuck in the same damn spot. "I can't afford to piss off Black. No one has done anything to me. The guy didn't hurt me, Sean, and I'm a call girl. I did my job." *Yeah, keep telling yourself that Avery. You don't feel violated. Of course not.* I'm having trouble swallowing that lie. "I'll just head home and—" My phone chirps, so I fish it out of my pocket and look down at the screen.

There's a message from Marty:

Better sit down, Avery. Saw this and thought you should know. It's bad. People recognize you. Call if you want to talk.

Sean and Mel are arguing, but their voices turn to noise as apprehension fills my stomach. I press the link and a video starts. Mortified, I look away and try not to cry. One of the videos from the other night—a full body shot of me pleasuring myself—is online. Being a call girl for Black is one thing. I'm a whore, but no one else knew about it. I could live with that, sort of, but this is unthinkable. Without blinking, I shove the phone at Sean and walk away. My feet move down the tree-lined street as horror rises up and drowns me. I don't realize how hard I'm trying not to cry until I feel Sean's hand on my shoulder. I stop in my tracks and turn, unable to look him in the eye.

Sean doesn't speak. He takes me in his arms and holds me against his chest, tangling his hands in my hair as he comforts me. My throat is so tight that I can't swallow. I can't breathe. There have already been hundreds of views and the video hasn't even been there for a whole day. My mind is collapsing brick by brick.

When Sean speaks, his voice has a deep gentleness about it that makes me want to believe every word he says. "I'll take care of it. That will be gone within the hour. Avery, listen. I need you to tell me everything. I'll fix this, and make it so the guy who fucked with you will wish he'd never been born."

CHAPTER 2

"You want me to do what?" Mel snaps at Sean with her hands plastered firmly to her curvy hips. The girl is wearing sweatpants and still looks gorgeous. It's amazing. Come to think of it, Mel is amazing, period. She goes to class, does her work, turns in papers, has high test scores, and manages to live this double life, all without breaking a nail. The job doesn't seem to bother her. I wonder how much of that is an act? It's hard to jump out of the center of a raging river without any help. Most people just drown, but Mel keeps going. She's close to the end and we both know it.

Sean's voice has the soft, patient tone that means he's ready to lose it and go nutso on her ass. "Drive back to the dorm and leave Avery with me. When people ask where she is, tell them that she came back with you. If someone's keeping an eye on her, I want them watching the dorm and not looking for her here."

Mel folds her arms over her chest while Sean speaks and then sighs dramatically. "So, what? You can mess with her head even more? I can take care of Avery, okay. I got skills." Mel works her jaw as she stares him down.

Sean steps into Mel's space. Her arms drop to her sides and her fingers flex, ready to throw a punch. I step forward and try to interrupt, but Sean talks over me. Glaring at her, he snaps, "Someone is trying to hurt her. There are enough people who'd want to do it that I can't even venture a guess at who it might be, which is why they need to think she has no clue. That means we should make it look like she heads back to New York with you. Actually doing that would be the height of stupidity."

Mel is ready to explode. "You don't know jackshit about me. I can throw a knife—"

He cuts her off. "I don't doubt that you can. And I don't question your ability to defend Avery—or yourself—if you know where the attacker is and what he plans to do, but we don't. Those variables are hidden at the moment, and having two people watching her back is better than having one. When it comes to a knife fight, my money's on you, but this isn't that kind of fight. Someone is manipulating her, trying to move Avery into a position that's still unclear. If they wanted to physically hurt her, they would have done it already. That's not what this is about."

"You think I can't outsmart someone?"

Sean is practically growling. If he was a dog, his hackles would be raised and he'd be flashing his fangs. "Why do you have to be so argumentative? Don't you want to keep her safe?"

"Why do you think that you can do a better job than me?" Mel is on her toes, yell-screaming in his face. "I've kept her safe until now."

Sean blinks and looks surprised. "You did?"

Mel's jaw drops and she's quiet for half a beat. Then she pushes a finger to the center of his chest. "Damn straight, I did. I did a bunch of stuff that you don't have a clue about because you weren't there, Ferro. You and your fucked up shit were somewhere else, nailing some other call girl."

Sean's gaze is lethal. For a moment he says nothing. A breeze moves through the trees, rustling the leaves and blowing Sean's dark hair. He relaxes as if he's lost the fight and then throws the killing verbal punch. "I see. Remind me again who introduced her to Miss Black in the first place?" Mel's entire body starts shaking and her mouth opens like she wants to scream, but Sean's voice is soft and careful, which is rare for him. It makes Mel freeze in place, like a banshee about to wail. "Two people watching out for Avery is better than one."

Mel snaps her mouth shut and she tucks her hands into the crooks of her arms. "Fine, but I hate you."

"As long as you take care of Avery, I respect you."

"Awh, fuck." Mel drops her arms to her sides like a pouty little kid. "You can't be nice to me, Ferro. What the hell was that?"

"The truth." Sean glances at me, like he doesn't know what to do with me. "Avery's friendships are questionable at best. Everyone has something on her, except you. If people find out what she does, you go down with her. I don't extend trust often, so don't blow it."

I expect Mel to go all cray cray on his ass, but she just rolls her eyes. "Like your trust matters to me, tightey whitey. I'm done with this conversation." She turns to me, "Avery, you'll have to put up with this loser for a little while longer. Don't do something stupid while I'm gone. And if you decide to give him that ring, you should shove it up his ass." She walks away muttering obscenities. I can tell she likes Sean, a little, but still thinks he's more trouble than he's worth.

"Uh, Mel," I call after her. She gives me a super-irritated look after turning around. Giving her a half smile, I hold up my keys. "You need these. And when I get back, we can hit IHOP. Promise."

Mel snatches the key ring from my hand. There's a unicorn on it from when I was in seventh grade. My mom gave it to me after Missy Walker humiliated me in the girl's locker room. My boobs were virtually nonexistent then, and Missy made sure everyone knew it.

There's a story my mom told me, about seeing through the surface and recognizing the magic that lies beneath. No one notices that the white animal is a unicorn at first. They see a snowy mare and nothing more. It isn't until you really look at the thing that you see its horn. It's transparent and gleams against the silver plate, and it's the kind of thing a person misses if they look quickly.

My mom taught me to look beyond the surface and I can't help but smile because Mel is like that. On the outside, she's beauty and fire, fang and tooth. She'll rip a person to shreds for the fun of it. At least it seems that way at first. It isn't until you spend time with her that it becomes clearer that she's been hurt beyond repair and that her nature is protective more than anything else.

We're all like that, all three of us. We've been destroyed by this life. The thing is, I don't want it to be over. I don't want to resign, dig my grave, and jump in. As long as there's still air in my lungs, I want my life back. I want to have a family again. I want to love and be loved. I refuse to keep treading water, because it's getting me nowhere. Day by day, I grow wearier and I'm sick of it. I want to live again and I know the path to that life lies with these two friends.

Mel rubs her thumb over the metal unicorn. She smiles and shakes her head at me, like she knows me better than she should. "You know I love me some pancakes. And Avery—everything is going to work out." Her voice catches in her throat when she says it, like she knows worse things will be coming.

CHAPTER 3

I'm stuck inside the house, watching the construction crew for a few hours, before Sean shoves a helmet on my head and tells me to get on the back of his bike.

I take it off, jump to my feet, and follow him outside to where his motorcycle is parked at the curb. Shoving the helmet back at him, I say, "I'm not taking your only helmet."

Sean's eye twitches slightly before he rubs his hands over his face to hide the tic. I'm not being annoying enough to cause that, but Sean seems to think so. "Then what do you suggest?"

"That you put it on, so you don't have to wear scrambled brains on your shoulders for the rest of your life. If you add a face that's been smeared like roadkill to that growling and eye-twitchy thing you got going on, well, people will talk, Sean, dear."

Sean glances up at me, cocking an eyebrow. "When did I growl?"

"Not right now, but you do it frequently when someone pisses you off and since everyone pisses you off—" I shrug my shoulders.

"Avery, what's it going to take to get your ass on this bike?" I'm quiet for a moment. My mind is still stuck on the fact that Sean growls at people, but he doesn't make that noise in the bedroom. He must read my thoughts, because his annoyed pout turns into a sultry smirk. "Avery, stop thinking about sex."

My jaw drops. "I was not!"

"You were too. Your eyes get this doe look before you space out and fail to answer important questions." Sean is straddling the bike, and I have no recollection of when he got on. My eyes can't help but rove over his jeans which are hugging his thighs. I'd love to feel those thighs around me again, but I won't do it. I know whatever we had is done, unless I want to be his mistress—and I don't.

I won't settle. If I do, I'll be stuck in limboland, pining over some guy who isn't courageous enough to try again, and I can't fathom being paired with Sean if he feels that way.

I mean, the man is amazing, but I'm not happy staying like this. I want to move on, and it seems like he's content to stay stuck. I don't pretend to know what it's like to lose a spouse and a child. I can't imagine what Sean felt sitting through the trial that followed their deaths, either. Is it bad that I want Sean to let go of that? Can't he hold onto the good and let go of the bad?

I smile to myself, because it sounds so simple, but it's fucking hard. If I could separate the good memories from the bad, then I wouldn't be talking to my parents' tombstone when things get bad. I'd be able to accept that they're gone and look back at the time we had together with joy instead of gut-wrenching remorse.

I'm a hypocrite. How can I expect Sean to let go of his demons when I visit mine on a weekly basis?

I sit down hard on the curb and let out a sigh. Staring at the spokes, I ask, "So, why'd you buy Peter a house here? I can't picture you living in a place like this. I mean, I assume you like it since you bought it for him. At least on some level, but this is the kind of house that I'd want to grow old in, not you. I can't imagine the bad-ass Sean Ferro with little flower gardens and a sweet Cape Cod with white gingerbread trim on a tree-lined street." I place my hands on my stomach and lay back on a patch of grass and smile up at the sky.

"Are you wondering if you chose the wrong Ferro?" There's a teasing tone in his voice, but it's laced with a tension that tells me he really wants to know.

I don't look over at him. I know he's sitting on his bike, looking like a modern god with that toned body, tight dark shirt, and the perfect dusting of stubble on his strong jaw. "No. I chose the right guy, he just didn't choose me back."

"Avery—"

Smiling, I say, "No, Sean. It's the truth and it's something that I need to realize. There's no future for us. You've been saying that from day one, but I didn't listen. I thought I could change you, or that you'd come around, but this house proves it—it shows how different we are and differences like that can't be changed. They're too big. The chasm is too wide. The only thing that moving forward will ensure is that one of us ends up at the bottom of the ravine, smashed to bits, and I seriously doubt I'm up for that right now." Plus, I know I can't fly and I'm not so stupid that I'd try.

Sean slips off his bike and sits next to me. He doesn't lay back and look at the way the leaves dapple the light and cast lacy shadows on the ground. I'd never expect him to even notice. It's not that Sean's oblivious, that's not it. It's more that he only pays attention to the important things in life. *He's paying attention to you*, the little voice inside my head whispers. I tell her that she's stupid and shove her back into the closet at the back of my head. She'll have me picking out a wedding dress if I listen to her ideas. Idiot.

To my surprise, Sean leans back in the grass and asks, "What are we looking at?"

A smile spreads across my lips. I can't hide how much it means to me. "My future. I want a house with a big maple tree and a grassy lawn. I want to lay on it in the summer and feel the blades of grass between my fingers and toes. I want the sensation of the cool dirt on my back as I try to figure out where the sky ends and the heavens begin. I want a toddler that runs out and jumps on my stomach, begging me to play. I want to take him to the beach and kiss his little toes." My smile fades as I look over at him. "Do you ever feel like your life is right in front of you, but you have no idea how to step into it? I mean, it's right there. There's a guy that's crazy about me who offered me all of these things and I said no." I said no. I didn't give that guy a chance. Marty wants the same things I do. That match would have made sense, and stepping into that life would be easy.

Sean stiffens because he knows exactly who I'm talking about. "I thought you didn't feel like that toward Marty?"

I shrug. "Does it matter how I feel? He's a great guy and we have fun together. I know he'd take care of me and give me everything I could ever want." I speak to the branches at the base of the massive tree, wondering how horrible it would be to marry Marty. I'd get the house and the kids. I could have my life without being a call girl. Marty would take me in a heartbeat. I know he would. Turning my face to the side, I look at Sean. "Does it bother you to hear?"

He's quiet for a moment and then swallows hard. "I didn't realize that he was so serious about you."

"He is. The guy is larger than life. He doesn't do things small and I can't help but notice that Marty wants me the way I want you. It's easy to see. Irony's a bitch, huh? Or is that karma? Either way, I'm screwed no matter how you look at it. The guy I want doesn't want me, and the guy that wants me, well, he doesn't compare to you."

Sean's voice is flat. "I ruined your life."

Smiling softly, I glance over at him. "No, you didn't." Sean makes a face that says he doesn't believe me. "No, seriously, you made it better. You made me see that I can choose to stay where I am or try to claw my way out. I plan on clawing, and it would have been nice if you were somehow factored into that equation, but I'll take what I can get. That's the way the world works. Besides, I'd rather have you as a friend than nothing at all."

Sean takes my hand in his, and the both of us lay there for a while as buddies. *Amigos. Compadres.* I can totally do this. I can ignore the sinking feeling in my stomach and the way my arm tingles because he's holding my hand. Everything doesn't have to be sexual, even though I want him that way. I won't think about the fact that Sean didn't correct me, that he didn't say our relationship is nothing like mine and Marty's, and that it's not completely lopsided. No, I won't think of any of those things. I'll lay here and hold his hand, because that's what he's offered—his friendship.

Yeah. Being stuck in the friend zone sucks.

CHAPTER 4

Sean takes my new helmet and puts it on the desk. We're in his tiny hotel room, which is nothing like the nice suite we had back in New York. I'm exhausted and flop down on the only bed. It looks like a double, which totally sucks. I guess I'm sleeping on the floor.

Sean sits on the edge of the mattress, by my feet. "You can shower first. I'll—" he stops talking and pulls his phone from his pocket. It buzzes again. Someone is texting him. Sean looks down at his phone and grimaces. "Okay, scratch that." He smashes his lips together hard and glances over at me with a completely conflicted look.

He curses and sends a text back before saying, "I need to go take care of something. If I leave you here to take a shower, will you actually take a shower? Or will you leave the room as soon as I walk away?"

My mouth opens and my cheek twitches. An offended sound that has a lot of hard k's scrapes the back of my throat before I manage to spit out, "I'm not an idiot." My hands do this little loop-d-loop thing when I say it, which looks very idiotic but I'm too tired to care.

Sean pinches the bridge of his nose, saying, "You sexted with someone and didn't bother to confirm their identity."

Wow. Thanks. "Harsh much?" I glare at him, giving him my best evil eye, but Sean doesn't look at me. "By the way, I did confirm the guy's identity. How was I supposed to know that he lied?"

Sean doesn't state the obvious. Yeah, I skipped that part of the whole sexting experience. Fine, I'm an idiot and he's too nice to say it to my face. Running his hands through his hair, Sean sighs and looks down at me. I'm still lying on the bed with my hands behind my head. "Avery, someone is gunning for you. This is serious, so please stay in the room. Don't talk to anyone, don't call anyone, and don't do anything until I get back. Promise me?"

"How long will you be gone?" I sit up and try to hide the worry I'm feeling. I didn't expect Sean to leave me alone. Picking at my nail polish, I add, "I'm a little nervous." I hated admitting that part, especially because it makes the turmoil Sean is feeling about leaving me ten times worse.

"I can't bring you with me or I would. I swear, I would." He's glancing down at me, but I don't look at him. Sean leans over, taking my face in his hands. My pulse skyrockets as my skin burns under his hands. A current of sparks shoots through my stomach and into my chest, stealing my breath. It's not fair that his touch conjures so much. I want to make Sean so lust ridden that he can't think. I want him to growl, whoop, or do whatever he does when he's lost in the moment. It's a luxury that he has denied himself, and I wish so badly that I could give it to him.

Sean's voice is tight when he speaks again. "Stay here. I'll be back as soon as I can. It should be before morning." He releases my cheeks and gives me a lopsided smirk. "You can sleep on the bed."

"Were you going to make me sleep on the floor?" I sit up and watch him pull his jacket on and pick up his helmet.

"Of course. What guy wouldn't want a beautiful woman at his feet?" He laughs and the sound makes me smile.

I smack his thigh, as if he offended me, but he didn't. Instead my mind derailed into Dirtyville again and I start thinking about what kind of things I could do to him if I were at his feet.

"Stop it, Avery." Sean laughs and shoves me. I fall sideways onto the bed.

"I wasn't thinking about you!"

"Yeah, right. I know you weren't thinking about Marty. Or Mel."

Raising my arm, I hold up a finger, like I'm making an important point while my face is still half buried in a pillow. "I'm not batting for that team."

"Which makes me really happy." Sean is at the door and turns back to me. "I'll bring dinner when I come back. No sexting. No clients. No Miss Black, and no anything."

I nearly choke. Pushing up on an elbow, I scoff, "No clients? You seriously think I'd take a client while you were gone? Sean!"

Straight-faced, he says, "I was talking about me." He winks and disappears through the door before I have a chance to hit him with my shoe.

He's teasing me. I know what he's doing, and it won't work because I refuse to have sex with him again. But that doesn't mean that I can't screw with him a little bit. There's a new flat screen TV across from the bed. I glance at my phone and back at the TV as an idea forms.

CHAPTER 5

The bed is hard and the room is dark, except for the flickering light of the TV. I've listened to my sexting videos too many times to count. I put them on an endless loop to mess with Sean when he comes back, but he hasn't showed yet and the damn videos are just making me horny. Plastering a pillow over my head, I roll over and try to muffle the sounds of video-me coming again.

I don't know how much time has passed, but I must have dozed off because I never heard the door open. A hand lands on my bare shoulder and before I can see anything, I throw a punch and yelp.

My wrist is caught in a vicelike grip before it collides with Sean's face. He watches me as I try to cut through the sleep induced haze. Words tumble out of my mouth before my brain checks them, "There are no hams!" Yeah. I don't think that made sense. What the hell was I dreaming about? I blink again and try to yank my wrist away, but Sean doesn't let go.

"Hams?" He laughs, and then sits on the side of the bed. "Don't worry, I'm not here to take your hams, Miss Smith. However, after viewing this little treat you left for me on the TV, I might be interested in sampling some of your other goods."

"Psh!" I throw a punch with my other hand and he grabs that one too. Sleepily, I blink at him and yawn, "I shoulda thought this through." Sean has both my wrists and looks like he plans on devouring me. We never ate dinner. I'm allowed to dream of pork and bacon. Bacon would be good. "I don't think you want to mess with a sleepy girl and her hams."

"What the hell were you dreaming about?"

"Like it matters? I'm never going to hear the end of this, and every time I eat ham, I'm going to be aroused because of that stupid video."

Sean laughs so hard that I feel like the funniest person alive. Score. I'm amusing. It isn't until he tugs my wrists to his chest and leans in close to my ear that I notice a spattering of something on his shirt. Since this is Sean, I doubt that it's ketchup. Why does he have blood on his shirt? Did he get into a fight? What the hell was he doing?

Sean's voice has that husky tone that makes me crazy. "I loved that video. I wish you made it for me."

"I did. Sorta."

Sean lingers close to my lips and releases a slow breath. It makes me close my eyes. Every ounce of me wants to lean into him and let Sean do anything he wants, but this has to stop. When his lips touch the side of my face I nearly jump out of my skin. Sucking in a sharp breath, I try to pull away, but he doesn't let me. Sean's mouth drifts to my neck, one hot kiss at a time, and my resolve starts to soften. When did I become so easy?

"Sean…" I manage to say his name, but it sounds too breathy, like I want him to keep going. So I try again. "Wait."

His grip on my wrists loosens as his face tips up from my neck. "Using the TV like that was cheating. I can hardly control myself around you, Avery. Do you know how hard it is to look at you and not touch you? When you laid on the grass today, it took every ounce of restraint to keep from taking you right there." My face burns at the thought. I can't help it. Sex in public places makes me bashful. Sean smashes his eyes closed before looking at me again. "Oh God, don't do that. You're killing me. How am I supposed to be around you and not have you? I'm so hard it hurts, Avery. I need you."

He presses me back into the bed and I feel how badly he wants me through his jeans. Sean presses his hands between my thighs, pushing my legs apart, and lays in between, rocking his hard body against mine. Since Mel drove off with all my clothes, I'm only wearing panties and a tee shirt, so there's very little keeping us apart. Deep inside, my body reacts to him and pulsates. The heat between my legs demands his presence. I want him on me, in me, and the slow grinding is making me lose my mind. The video was such a mistake. I would have been able to tell him no easily before, but now I'm half asleep and very aroused. Plus, it's Sean. His scent fills my head as he rocks against me and holds my wrists to the bed. How'd I end up on the bottom?

Sean leans in for a kiss, and it kills me, but I manage to turn my face to the side. He lingers, allowing his hot breath to move across my skin before backing up. "Tell me."

It's such a simple request, two words and no more, but I can't do it. Besides, what am I supposed to say? 'I'm over you, Sean Ferro. Go away.' Like that'll ever happen. I'm not over him at all and I'm rather thrilled to be under him at the moment. Fuck. I'm so mental. "I want you, but…"

Sean grins and backs off, sitting down beside me. Rubbing his hands over his face, he sighs. "Now you have morals?"

Darting upright in the bed, I'm wide awake and ready to chew him out. "Excuse me? I've always had morals!"

Sean glances over at me, like he's trying not to laugh. "Are you serious? You signed up to be a call girl. If you didn't walk into Black's and sign on the line—"

"I'd already met you by the time I did that. I saw your picture, and then I signed." Oh shit. That didn't sound right. My face scrunches as I turn away from him and try to hide under the sheet.

Sean swats the thin fabric away. The lights aren't on and the TV is still playing that video. I can see my splayed legs behind his head, glowing like a pair of sexy antlers. "Come again?" he says, leaning closer to me. "Did you just say that the only reason you became a call girl was to get dates?"

"No!"

"Then what was it?"

"To sleep with you, loser. Weren't you listening?" I shove his arm, hard, but Sean barely moves. "I have morals. I do. I'm a very moralistic person." Sean's smiling at me and has a funny look on his face. It makes me squirm. I can't tell what he's thinking at all and that concerns me. I push his shoulder again, and say, "Stop it."

"I'm sorry. I stand corrected. You have morals. They're a very strange set of idealistic codes, but you have them. Apparently I'm the only one in this relationship who is devoid of scruples."

"You're not devoid of anything. You just put them away for a while." I look down at my hand when I notice the reddish sticky substance on my palm. It wasn't there before I shoved him. There's more blood on his sleeve. My eyes flick up and lock with his blue gaze. Holding up my hand, I ask, "Is this blood? Tell me that you didn't kill someone tonight. Because I'm pretty sure this isn't yours."

Sean takes my bloody palm and pulls me off the bed. "I didn't kill anyone. Someone was... You know what, forget it. It's taken care of and I'd like to help you clean this off, if you'll let me." There's a question in his tone.

I don't like this. I don't know where he went or what he did. There are a few spatters of something dark on his shirt, at least it only seems like a few, but I can't see very much with the lights out. Maybe I don't want to know, and at the same time I do, because if Sean kicked someone's ass it assures me that he can take care of me no matter what happens.

I nod. It's all the approval Sean needs.

CHAPTER 6

He nods curtly and heads to the bathroom to turn on the shower. When he returns, he walks toward me like he knows exactly what he plans to do. Sean's hands reach for the hem of my shirt, where they pause as he looks up into my eyes. My breath catches in my throat as my heart explodes, racing even faster than before. Not knowing what he's doing, combined with that look, knocks the breath out of me. I can barely stand as he strips me.

First, the shirt comes over my head and I fold my arms over my chest. I don't mean to do it, but I can't help myself. Sean is intimidating when he has this look in his eyes. It's like he's found a mouse to bat around and plans to keep the poor creature in play long enough to take what he wants. There's a carnal side to him that scares me, because I know what he wants—what he needs. Sean's taken it from me before and doing that again terrifies me. I wonder exactly what I just gave him permission to do.

Sean's thumbs hook into the sides of my panties, as his eyes rake over the swells of my breasts, half hidden by my arms. He slips the fabric over my hips, making me suck in a sharp breath as he tugs them.

Why can't I tell him no? I can tell Marty no. No. Say it, Avery! Tell him that he can't have you! But I want him. And that's the truth. I want this to be real so badly that I'm willing to pretend, even if it's for a little while. Maybe I'm not totally mental, I mean stripping isn't the same as sex and he's already seen me naked. This body should be old news to him, right?

Based on the look on Sean's face, this body will never be old news. I like how he makes me feel. Goddesses would blush if he looked at them like that. Those blue eyes, that wicked smirk, and the way he's so close but not close enough—Sean Ferro makes me totally crazy.

Sean kneels in front of me as he slowly slips my bottoms down over my thighs. He's right in front of me, close enough to do all sorts of naughty things with his face right there. I'm utterly still as I shift my weight, foot to foot, and he pulls my panties off. Sean wads them in his hand and lifts them to his face before breathing in deeply. This time when his eyes flash upward, I can't breathe at all. His look shoots through my body and into my core in a single, hot streak. Dirty thoughts fly through my mind without caution. I hope he grabs my ass hard and pulls the V at the top of my legs to his face, so he can lick me generously, from ass to clit. While he's still on his knees, I picture him burying his face in my lower lips, licking and sucking my sensitive skin, driving his tongue deeper and deeper inside me, while he pulls my hips down hard, as if he can't get enough. My entire body is trembling, watching Sean, waiting to see what he'll do.

But the sexy man doesn't do those things. Instead, he rises from the floor and reaches for me, taking my hands from my breasts. His eyes don't lift from my chest, where my nipples are tightening into hard little nubs. Heart racing, I manage to stand there and let him stare, but the aching in my breasts—the desire to touch and be touched—worsens.

The way he's breathing makes me yearn for his hands on my flesh. My skin is so sensitive, so ready to be felt, but Sean remains still, standing there looking at me like he's never going to see my body like this again.

His eyes slip over every curve, memorizing all of me, until his chin tips up. "I've never seen anyone as beautiful as you, and it amazes me that you still try to cover yourself, like you don't know how desirable and perfect your body truly is. Don't hide from me, Avery. Not tonight. I won't touch you. I won't do anything you don't want me to."

I can't find my voice, so I nod, and get treated to a light smile. His eyes travel up and down my body again, and I wish they were his hands. Or his lips and that sinful tongue. Long, wet licks sound about right. I'm too tired to think and too lusty to stand there like I'm not. His eyes fixate on my right breast and I wonder if that's his favorite. The question floating through my mind falls out of my mouth without much thought. "If you could lower your lips to any place on my body, but you only had one kiss, where would you choose?"

Sean looks at me through those dark lashes and smiles. "May I show you?"

The giddy part of me that's turned into a lust ridden siren replies, "Yes."

I wonder what he's going to do, because Sean hesitates. His eyes drop to my nipples, one at a time, and then he steps back, looking me over. Sean circles me once, slowly, making my heart slam into my ribs even harder. The place between my legs is so hot, and throbbing hard. I want him so badly and I'm hoping he picks some place really racy to kiss me. His lips pressed between my thighs would be heaven. That mouth on my breast, sucking and teasing me into oblivion sounds delicious, too.

Sean stops in front of me and looks down into my face. Lowering his head slowly he presses his mouth to mine. The heat from his lips bursts into flames when the kiss connects. I want to grab his head with my hands and pull his hair, but I keep my hands plastered to my sides. This is his kiss and I want to see what he does, so I don't move.

Sean kisses me again, gently pressing against me. Sean's bottom lip catches mine and he nips me lightly before sliding his tongue over the seam of my mouth. I part my lips for him, but Sean doesn't kiss me that way. It's the most innocent, chaste kiss he's ever given me. When Sean pulls away I nearly fall over. I rasp, like someone sucker-punched me, and stare at him.

He doesn't explain what he did or why. Sean simply extends his hand and says, "Come on, Miss Smith. I need to clean you up and get you to bed."

I slip my palm into his and follow him into the bathroom. He helps me into the shower, but doesn't give me a washcloth or soap. "Rinse off and call me when you're ready."

"Ready for what?" My voice barely comes out.

Sean makes an amused sound as he tugs the curtain closed. Uh, I didn't think I was funny just then, but okay.

I let the water pound my face and my back, but I'm strung so tight that I'll never sleep, not now. Not with Sean here. After a few moments, I decide against giving myself a good time. With my luck, he'll walk in on me and that would be completely mortifying. Doing it in front of someone is different than doing it on camera. There's separation, and it didn't feel as dirty. Maybe I should just go to sleep. I do want soap though, and a soft pillow sounds nice, especially if my loins simmer down, so I call him.

Sean returns without his shirt, but he's still dressed. I can't hide my disappointment, but I try. Apparently, I do a shitty job. Sean smiles at me. "Hoping for something else?" I shrug. "I hate it when you do that. Say something. Own it. Tell me what you're thinking, what you're hoping for. I want to hear."

"You don't like it when I shrug? That's an old man thing to say. You can't say stuff like that," I tease. I figure that I look like a drowned rat, but Sean's gaze says something else. Drowned rats aren't fuckable and his eyes say that I am. If he gave me a bar of soap I would have dropped it and bent over just to see what he'd do. No wonder he took the soap away.

Reaching forward, he wets a washcloth before putting soap on it. "Hands," he says, and I give them to him, holding them out like he's going to handcuff me. Sean flips them over and washes each one carefully, while he speaks. "I am old. Besides, you know your mind. I wish you weren't so afraid to speak it."

I nearly double over with laughter. "You think that's the problem? That I don't want to tell you what I think? I can tell you. Believe me, that's not it."

"Okay," he says, as he abandons the washcloth and dumps more shower gel into his hands, "tell me where you wanted me to kiss you before." His palms land on my upper arms and work the gel into a lather. Oh my God, it feels good.

"I don't know. I hadn't decided. Either right breast or, uh—"

"Say it." His voice is commanding, like he'll whip me if I don't confess this second.

"Between my legs?" Why did that sound like a question?

Sean smirks as his hands rub soap over my stomach and up to my ribs. "I can get you to say exactly what you're thinking without any hesitation at all. I just—"

That makes me laugh. "No you can't. That's a bunch of bullsheeee." My voice jumps an octave when his fingers wrap around my nipples and squeeze. My chin drops and I squeal as my back arches toward his hands. The touch is pure agony because he keeps his distance on the other side of the tub. I can't rock my hips against his and there's no outlet for the torture between my legs.

"What were you saying?" Sean smiles devilishly as water splashes up onto his bare chest. The only thing I can think about is licking each drop off with my tongue. I have no idea what he was talking about. "Oh, yes, tell me where you wanted my mouth during that kiss." He rubs his fingers, pressing gently, watching my eyes as he does.

My mouth opens into a wide O and I squeak. "Between my legs."

He shakes his head. "Not good enough." His fingers clamp down like vices on my tender flesh.

Gasping, I try to pull away from him, but it just makes it worse. Pleasure and pain responses are firing through my brain like a lightning storm. He needs to let go or do more to sate my lust. Sean catches my eye and is watching me closely. I know he likes to see the pain dancing across my face, but he doesn't take things too far. Not this time.

I'm making noises that will haunt me in daylight, and am close to hopping—what's that about?—but I don't answer him the way he wants, so he starts to twist. Oh. My. God. Suddenly the shower feels like fingers all over my skin and I gasp again and again as he tightens his grip. Coils of heat shoot through my core and my knees buckle, but Sean doesn't allow me to dip. He holds me in place by my breasts, with his dark eyes on my face, fixated, and expressionless.

"Tell me," he commands, as his hands twist both nipples in the same direction while increasing the pressure. I want to say it. I do, but I can't talk like that when I'm not in the heat of the moment. It's wrong or something. But my poor tatas are going to be stuck in a corkscrew shape if I don't talk soon. "Say it." He commands me again and twists the other way, increasing pressure as he does so.

"Pussy!" I blurt out. "I wanted you to kiss my pussy and lick me--hard." The last word catches in my throat. I don't look up at him. Saying stuff like that, out loud, to Sean, is unthinkable. I'm caught between pleasure and pain, somewhere between heaven and hell, with this beautifully twisted man watching streams of water flow over my body.

Sean doesn't show any emotion, instead he slowly untwists my nipples and eases up on the pressure, but he doesn't let go. I glance up at him. As if he can read my mind, he explains, "It'll hurt more if I just let go."

"More than before?"

He nods and then asks, "Why can't you just take what you want?"

I can't shrug because his hands are still on my breasts, holding me. "Why do you have to manipulate me? Why can't you just say you want to fuck me?"

"Because I don't want to fuck you." He releases more pressure and then let's go. Those blue eyes burn like twin flames.

My breasts ache because of what he did and because he's gone. "Yeah, you want to own me. I got it and I'm not for sale. Well, I am, but that's more like renting than buying me." I have no idea what I'm saying. I'm mad he did that and angry that he got a confession that was so deep, so fast, and then he says he's not interested.

I lift my hand to slap him in the face. Every single time the man grabs my wrist and stops me, but not this time. There's a loud crack when my wet palm lands on his cheek. His sapphire eyes stare at me without remorse as I slip my hand away. "I don't want to buy you. I don't want to fuck you. Ask me why, Avery."

I'm trembling, wondering what came over him. The water is hot, but I shiver anyway and look away. "No." I can't fathom why or what he wants. Not after everything we've been through. I want to cry. He doesn't want me at all anymore? He just wants to cause me pain? I can't deal with this.

"No?" He sounds shocked. "You can't say no."

"Yes, I can and I just did." He's looking at me like he wants to throw me through the wall. I plaster my arms across my nipples so he can't make me say anything else I'll regret.

Sean's gaze drops for a moment. When he looks back up, his eyes flash. "If that's the way you want it."

I've won. He's backing down. Sean turns around and opens the bathroom door. He's leaving, but then he turns back and grins wolfishly before stepping into the shower with me. I screech as the water sprays everywhere. It streams down his cheeks and plasters his hair to his face, as Sean presses my back into the cold tile wall.

Sucking in a sharp breath, I try to move, but he pins me. "Ask me why." His eyes search mine and I'm no longer sure what he's going to say. "Ask me why I don't want a fuck, or why I don't want to buy you. Ask me why I don't want to share you with Black or anyone else. Ask me why my dick is hard and I'm still wearing pants, pressing my body against the most beautiful woman in existence. Ask me why she's naked and I'm not. Ask me, Avery. Ask me anything. I'm begging you." There's a soft plea in his voice that nearly breaks me, but I can't bear to hear his answer.

I don't want to talk and I'm afraid of what he has to say, I'm afraid it's horrible and I can't take more bad news without falling apart. I want him to take me in his arms and pull me against his chest. I want to sleep with him beside me and pretend that my life isn't falling apart.

The question I ask eases the fear that's strangling me. Looking up into his eyes, I press my lips together and say, "Can you hold me?"

Sean pulls me into his arms and holds on tight. The water continues to pour over us, and he stays like that with me, until I ask to move to the bed. We crawl under the covers, Sean in boxers, and me totally naked. He wraps his arms around me and lets me nuzzle against his chest. I'm in forbidden territory and I don't know how I got here. Resisting the urge to touch, I close my eyes and try to sleep.

Something changed. I can feel it, I just don't know what.

CHAPTER 7

Sean needs to head out to Long Island and I manage to talk him into returning me to my dorm for an hour or so. My argument for doing so was ironclad. I have no clothes. No, he can't buy me more because I need some specific things—girl things for work—and they're in my dorm. Plus, I need my books and all the crap I photocopied for my term project. That thing is due at the end of the week.

Sean hesitates when we finally pull up in front of the dorm. "I don't like this Avery."

I slip off the back of his bike and shuck my helmet. My hair is plastered to my head and I'm sure I have that greasy used car salesman thing going on. "Sean, I know you're worried about me, but Mel is up there. And have you met Amber? Evil guys are afraid of hags. She's vile. No one will mess with me while the two of them are there. It's not like I'm walking down a dark alley alone, on Halloween, with an axe murderer on the loose. I'm not TSTL."

"What does that mean?"

"Too stupid to live." I don't mean to laugh, but I do. "What, do you live in a cave?" I make a roaring sound and claw a pretend paw at him. His head tilts to the side and he's ready to get off the bike. Pressing my hands to his, I add, "Seriously, Sean. Treat me like an adult even if I don't sound like one. If I don't take care of myself—at least a little bit—I'll go crazy. This is so minor. It's day time. It's a freakin' dorm."

Sean glances up at the building again and back at me. "Fine, but I'll come up with you." He puts his kickstand down and starts to turn off the bike, but I stop him.

"No, you're not. Sean, you have something to do. Go do it as fast as you can, and when you come back, I'll be packed and ready. You said you'd be right down the street. I can call you if I need help. I promise."

After a lot more groveling and pleading, Sean finally agrees to let me go inside by myself. He'll be back in a heartbeat if I need him, and he makes me swear to call him if something isn't right.

The truth is, nothing's right. Last night I laid in bed with him and it was perfect, in a surreal sort of way. I wasn't wearing a stitch of clothing and it wasn't weird. It didn't feel forced. I didn't care what I looked like. It was more about how I felt, and with Sean's strong arms around me, I felt good. It makes my stomach churn to think of the desperation in his eyes when he wanted me to ask him why I was out of bounds. I don't want to know. I can play make-believe a while longer, can't I?

When does pretending become a mental illness? I've had to pretend day in and day out that I'm fine, that I'm not falling apart. How is this any different? Sean's my friend. I can live with that. Sort of. It's unfair for me to expect more from him. Sean's the way he is for a reason. He isn't asking me to leave my baggage behind, not that I could. Besides, it's not really baggage. It's more like scars. Those don't go away no matter what kind of high priced goop you slather on them. Some people say scars build character, but I think they make weak points in my suit of armor and the more scars that appear over my heart, the more likely I am to skewer myself and never get up. There's no way to get through the day without that suit. Some people call that suit sanity, others call it the ability to deal with life. Either way, I know mine has been etched away, as if acid has been placed over my heart for years on end. The piece that protects my heart is paper-thin and too weak to protect me from much more.

For some reason, when Sean's around it doesn't feel that way. It feels like someone healed me and that constant aching at the center of my chest vanishes. The grief that strangles me in my nightmares is gone. I can sleep when he's next to me. There are no shadows pulling me into the icy waters and clawing at my hair until I stop struggling and drift beneath the waves.

And that's the thing. Life is a struggle. Who am I to complain because it isn't easy? Mel's life has been so much more horrifying and would have crushed a weaker person. I couldn't walk a foot in her shoes, never mind a mile. I don't know how she does it. I don't know how she finds laughter when there is none.

I'm pulled from my thoughts as the doorknob twists. I'm hunched over the sink, up to my elbows in bubbles. Expecting to see Amber, I speak over my shoulder, saying sarcastically, "Thanks for cleaning the room."

Translation: she didn't clean up anything. Her and one of her boinking buddies must have cooked something fishy on the hotplate and left it in the room all night. The smell when I came in was so bad that no amount of air freshener will cover the stench. I already bleached the dirty dishes and have been spraying Lysol since I got here. I'm pretty sure there's a cloud of disinfectant mist hovering in the center of the room like a tropical depression.

"You're welcome, but it's not my mess, babe. Amber had over that other guy she sees when I'm not around." Naked Guy is standing in the door way with low rise jeans and no shirt. It's still cold enough to snow.

I repress the urge to roll my eyes, and scrub a nasty pan in our little sink. Do you know how hard it is to clean pots and pans in a micro sink? Amber's an idiot. That's the first thought that enters my mind, and the second one is more alarming—what if it was him? Naked Guy is a few screws short. I shove my paranoia away, and say over my shoulder, "She's not here."

Naked Guy lets the door shut behind him and makes his way across the room to where I am. He leans against the counter opposite me and grins. "Oh? I guess she'll be here soon. Mind if I wait?"

Yes. "No. I'm leaving in a sec anyway. My friend is coming to pick me up. He's a big scary guy." Ha. I added that for good measure, but the dim wit doesn't seem to care. It so wasn't him. This guy couldn't find his way out of a barrel. He's too obsessed with his pecs.

I feel his eyes on the side of my face and know he's watching me. "So, are you and Amber going to the Astronomy Lab to watch the meteor shower this weekend? I heard it's supposed to look really cool from up there."

"Not my thing, babe. If a girl wants to see big rocks, I got a pair right here. 'Nuff said." He grabs his crotch as he pushes off the counter and steps closer to me, which makes the hairs on my arms stand on end. Ack, I can't stand him. What the hell does Amber see in this loser? Still holding the pan, I turn to look at him. There's a smile on his lips as his eyes dip to my chest, and then back to my face. Asshole. "But I don't think that's what you really want to talk about right now, is it? I mean, not after the other night."

I try not to react. That damn video was seen by way too many people, and they were happy to let me know it when I walked into the dorm. The girls nicknamed me 'slut,' which was very clever, and the guys let their eyes rove over my body in hope that I'd give them a second glance. I assume Naked Guy is in the ogling camp. What a jackass.

My eyes narrow to slits before I roll them. "Which night are you talking about? The one where you fucked my roommate and locked me out? Or the one where you two did it against the window so everyone in the quad could see?" I step toward him and press a finger to his chest, even though he towers over me. "Let's get one thing straight, my sexual life is none of your goddamn business and if you want to keep your head on your shoulders, you won't mention that video to me ever again." I turn back to the sink and scrub the pan so hard that the sponge tears.

Naked Guy steps in close behind me, which makes me way too nervous. It's paranoia, that's all. This guy couldn't hurt a flea. He acts like he's tough shit, but he's not. Mel's chased him out of here so many times. And every single time the dude ran away screaming like a girl. But this time, he doesn't run. I tense as I feel his breath on my neck. "Which video would that be, Avery? There were so many."

My body tenses and I clutch the pan like it's rope and I'm in a freefall. He's lying. There's no way he knows there is more than one clip. But then his phone is shoved under my nose and I see one of the other videos. Video-me is naked and breathing hard, ready to move the camera much lower.

Jutting my hand out, I try to grab the phone, but he doesn't let me. He holds it up high, just out of reach. The sponge goes flying and I'm left there, horrified, as my voice fills my ears. He cranks up the volume so I can listen to myself come.

I should call Sean.

I should kill Naked Guy and bury him under Amber's bed.

I need that phone. He can't have those videos.

I lunge at him again, and swing the pan at his head. Naked Guy shrieks in an octave way too high for a guy his size, "Whoa! You can't beat the shit out of me for being a paying customer. Miss Black wouldn't like that, would she?" His words don't register until I've taken two more swings. Both attempted whacks were wild and not thought out. He jumps out of the way and the pan connects with the counter, sending the remnants of the horribly loud DONG up my arm, which makes me madder.

"You bought me?" I hiss at him and crouch lower, holding the pan like a tennis racket.

Naked Guy looks less smug than a few moments ago. He nods, slightly. "Of course, but I was told you wouldn't care. Why are you freaking out?"

"Who said I wouldn't care?"

"Miss Black! She said you were a professional. I'm going to tell her that you're a raving psychobitch. You can't jerk off with me one night and then hit me with a fucking frying pan the next! What's wrong with you?"

"Why'd you upload that video?"

"Yeah, right. Like I'd do something like that? The videos are enough for me. When Black said you worked for her, I couldn't believe it. I told her that you act like a fucking nun, and of course I'd like to nail you. The sexting was a necessary evil, babe. I thought if you saw me, you'd walk out. So when you assumed I was someone else, I went with it. I mean, why not?"

Working my jaw, I bounce on the balls of my feet. I want to hit him so hard that his teeth fall out. "How'd the video get online?"

"How do you think?" he squeaks. "Amber. She saw it and thought we were having a thing. She might be a whore, but she's jealous." He laughs. "It's funny that you two room together. Do you guys do it when—"

"OHMYGODSHUTUP!" All the words run together as I piece together what happened. The pan lowers slightly and Naked Guy reads me wrong. I'm trying to figure out what the hell is going on, but he thinks it's an invitation for more. His hand touches my arm and the pan flies up and bangs into his wrist. "Do. Not. Touch. Me." I growl the words at him and he steps back cradling his arm.

"You didn't have to hit me!"

"How did you afford me? You're a leech." And this is the part that scares me. Naked Guy is broke. He bums stuff off his friends and lovers. He borrows money from Amber all the time, and helps himself to our food. He'd be wearing her clothes if they fit him.

He shrugs as his eyes dart to the side, following the movement of the frying pan as I tuck it under my arm. "I'm not totally broke, and I wanted to give you the chance to let it sink in before next weekend. I was being nice, Avery. But this Saturday, I won't be."

"What?" My voice barely comes out.

"I booked you, babe." He presses his finger to the tip of my nose and grins. "I told Miss Black that I wanted the kinkiest girl she has. Imagine my surprise when she showed me your picture. So, get ready for some serious fucking." He leans in and adds, "Because there are a few things that Amber won't do, and I'm so glad to hear that you'll do anything for the right price."

As he speaks, every muscle in my body tenses. My brain is telling my arm to swing the pan into his skull, even as I'm shaking. I don't know if it's fury, disgust, or betrayal, but I do it—I swing. The arm holding the pan flies up from my side and before Naked Guy can blink it connects with his shoulder. He's too tall. I missed.

His eyes narrow into thin slits after he bites back a scream. Advancing quickly, he rips the pan out of my hand and tosses it onto Amber's bed before taking my wrist and bending it behind my back. I fall to my knees as tears form in my eyes. Naked Guy pulls my arm in a direction that it doesn't want to go. I open my mouth to scream, but he covers it with his big hand. Leaning in close to my ear, he whispers, "You're going to pay for that." Yanking my arm hard, Naked Guy pushes me forward, releasing my arm as I let out a yelp and fall into the rug.

CHAPTER 8

When he turns around, something changes. I'm still doubled over, breathing hard, when I glance up and see Amber standing in front of Mel.

"Where the fuck is Ferro?" Mel says, rushing into the room. I tried to tell her I was back, but she wasn't in her room. Then the stench hit me and I forgot to text her. A knife appears in Mel's hand and she lunges at Naked Guy. "Get your filthy ass outa here right now!"

Naked Guy laughs at first, like she's kidding, and then turns on his heel and runs. He's out the door before Mel can stab him.

While Mel chases him down the hall, Amber walks over to help me off the floor. Placing her hand under my arm, she lifts me up onto my bed. "Are you okay?" I nod, not wanting to speak. My arm is aching and my head feels like it's going to split open.

How much did she hear? I want to bury my face in my pillows and cry. Or scream. How did he find Black? My mind is thinking in fragmented pieces. Nothing is stringing together. A high pitched shriek echoes from the quad below. I press my fingers to my temples and ask, "Did she stab him?" I hope not. That'll totally mess up everything she's been trying to fix.

Amber moves to the window and looks out. "No, Mel has him pinned to the ground, face-first, and is making him eat dirt." She laughs lightly. "You should come see." I walk over and look at the spectacle below. Mel has his face to the ground and is force-feeding him the lawn. The crowd watching is getting bigger, but Mel knows not to stay long enough for a teacher to walk over. She pushes up fast, kicks him in the side, and hurls a clump of grass at his head. Amber doesn't look at me. Instead she stares out the window at her boyfriend. "I didn't know he was like that, with you. I mean, I knew he slept around, but—"

"We didn't have sex," I blurt out. "I thought he was someone else or I wouldn't have sent him those messages. They were for this other guy." I take a deep breath and push my hair out of my face.

Amber doesn't lift her eyes from the window sill. "I'm sorry. I was the one who put the video online. I won't post any of the others." I nod, and don't look at her. For some reason, I'm not mad. I'm not really sure why. "So, it was a wrong number?" She sounds hopeful, like after what she just saw could be explained away.

"No, he knew it was me, Amber. And he would have broken my arm if you didn't walk in right then."

She nods, like she knows. "He has a temper."

Mel walks into the room and swats the dirt off her hands. There's a thin sheen of sweat on her face. "Where the fuck is Ferro? I thought you were with him and that's why I didn't need to be keeping an eye out for you. I'm gonna rip that boy a new—"

"Mel, stop. He dropped me off so I could grab my things. I told him to leave me."

"And he listened?" She plants her hands on her hips and gives me a how-dumb-is-he look.

"Who's Ferro?" Amber asks.

Mel lies, "Her cousin, Miss Nosey. And why did that piece of white trash have this?" Mel holds up a key. "He said you gave it to him."

Amber has a worried look in her eyes, but hides it quickly. "I did. It's my room, I can do what I want."

"No, you can't Dumber Than Dirt. Don't hand out keys or I'll take your ass and toss it out the window. Do we have an understanding?" Mel looks like she's ready to grab Amber right this second. When my roommate doesn't answer, Mel steps toward her.

The smug smile falls off of Amber's face and her hands dart up, palms out. "Fine! Don't touch me! I won't give out any more keys."

"Who else has a key?" I ask, concerned. Amber's an idiot, but I didn't realize part of her calling card included handing out copies of keys to our room.

Amber laughs nervously and shrugs her shoulders. "Your boyfriend."

Mel's caramel eyes cut to the side and meet mine before I ask, "Marty?"

Amber laughs, "Not the gay guy. The other one. He came by here looking for you a few times, wanting to celebrate something, but you weren't around. He gave me the bottle of champagne and left. I told him that you're working a lot and never around. He was trying to surprise you with a gourmet dinner and wine that cost more than my car," she shrugs, "so I gave him a key and told him that he could try to catch you late on a Thursday. It's the only day you're around anymore."

"Awh, fuck. Amber, how stupid are you?" Mel sounds pissed.

I just stand there and wonder if Amber is really trying to kill me or if she's that stupid. "So, you don't know his name? Or you won't tell me?"

"I don't remember. He told me, but I thought you only had one boyfriend! I was trying to help."

Glancing over at Mel, I ask, "Do you think it's Henry Thomas?"

She nods. When her gaze flicks back over to Amber, she asks, "Is there somewhere else you can stay?"

"You can't throw me out of my room!" Amber stands and pokes Mel in the chest.

One of Mel's dark eyebrows lifts as fairy-like laughter flutters out of her mouth, which sounds totally wrong. She swats at Ambers finger and growls, "It appears that you're too stupid to be here and since we're knee-deep in a real life horror movie, complete with psycho stalkers, I thought you might want to opt out before someone kills you."

Amber blinks her big eyes too many times. "What? That guy was a stalker?"

I nod and rub the heels of my hands over my eyes.

Sean chooses that moment to show up. His knuckles wrap the door and he pushes it open, peering inside. "What's wrong?"

Mel goes crazy on his ass for leaving me alone, while Amber tries to tell me something that I can't hear.

Sean finally holds up his hand, and yells, "Enough! Avery, get your things. We're leaving."

Mel is standing there like she wants to rip Sean's head off. "He had her pinned to the floor, Ferro. And where the fuck were you?"

"Too far away," he finally answers. Looking directly at Mel, he says, "It won't happen again, and thank you."

"For what?" Mel spits out.

"For pounding that guy into the ground. If I did it, well, let's just say it was better that you walked in and not me."

"Hmm. Meaning Naked Guy would be a smear by now." Mel nods and rolls her eyes, like Sean is all talk. The blood on his shirt the other night would suggest otherwise. I've wondered what that was about and what he did, but I'm very certain that it wasn't Sean's blood and that means I don't want to know. Mel reaches into her jean's pocket and hands me a piece of plastic.

"What's this?"

She grins. "Naked Guy's cell phone. I swiped it from him while I was kicking his ass."

CHAPTER 9

My eyes go wide as I clutch the phone in my hand. The screen is cracked, but it still works. I turn it on and find my videos. Oh thank god. I flick through and only see some of my pictures, and a few of the videos are missing. Glancing at Amber, I ask, "Where are the rest?"

For once Amber is helpful, and just answers the question. "I deleted them." She grins like a five year old in a candy store, showing way too many teeth. "What can I say? I'm the jealous type."

"Who knew," Mel snorts and shakes her head.

"I know, right?" Amber laughs and plops down on her bed. "He doesn't have copies anywhere. I asked."

"He could have lied to you," Sean says bluntly.

Amber shakes her head. "Not him. He likes to show off, and if he uploaded them to his computer in his dorm, let's just say that more videos would have shown up this morning. Plus, he tends to keep stuff like that on him at first because he doesn't like to share. Speaking of which, give me the phone." She holds out her hand, but no one hands it to her. Amber sighs dramatically. "My videos are on there too. I want to delete them before the asswipe posts them everywhere." I hand her the phone and let her find her files in silence.

Sean watches her and from the tension in his arms, I can tell that he wants to smash something. My nerves are totally gone and I feel like I'm going to lose it and burst into a ball of snot and tears. Amber tosses me the phone, which I hand to Sean. He pockets the thing and looks down at me. "Come on." He tilts his head toward the door, like I should automatically follow.

What am I? A dog? Woof. Here I come Sean. Pant. Pant. Fuck it. I fall into step behind him, and walk down the hallway with him and Mel. She's still pissed. I know how much she wants to bite his head off. Her jaw is locked and she finally comes unhinged in the stairwell.

"I don't trust you with her." Mel snaps as she stomps down the metal steps.

"No one asked you to." Classic Sean response, and like always, I'm caught in the middle.

"Guys, stop it." I'm so diplomatic. I could have ended the Cuban Missile Crisis in a day. Did you just see that massive about of diplomatic action? Sha'zoom! Yeah. Okay, I suck at stopping fights and I can tell that they're both brimming with stress and ready to kill anyone that steps into their path, including fuzzy bunnies. God save the bunnies.

They stop on the landing one floor down, ready to duel—verbally or with weapons—it's hard to say with these two. "You had one job, Ferro, and you left her alone! How fucking stupid are you?" Mel bites her lips as they curl into a sneer.

Sean faces off and steps directly in front of her. "You're not the only person who cares about her, so stop acting like you are. There was no way to know who was trying to hurt her."

"It was him, ass hat!" Mel yells and points up the stairs toward my room.

"Seriously, guys, cut it out." No one listens to me. I could toss my ass over the railing and jump. I wonder if I could grab one of the railings in a Spiderman fashion. I'd probably rip my arms off, which means Peter Parker is cooler than me.

Mel and Sean are in each other's faces, growling like rabid animals. I hate listening to people fight. It makes my mind wander down slightly insane routes, so I don't have to endure the yelling. My mom must have dropped me down a flight of stairs when I was a baby.

Awh, what the hell. I throw my leg over the metal railing and they don't notice until both feet are on the wrong side.

Sean turns and looks at me wide-eyed. "What are you doing?"

Mel glares at me like I've lost my mind. Maybe I have, because I'm afraid of heights and I don't really care that it's a long way down. "Get your scrawny ass back over here right now. I ain't even playing with you, Avery.

So help me God!" She actually stomps her foot. On me it would look ridiculous, but on Mel it looks scary. It probably has to do with the anger in her eyes and the fury on her face. Think Rumplestiltskin right before he fell through the floor. Hissy fit to the max, man.

"I hate this," I say, not looking directly at either of them. Instead, my eyes wander to the cement floor in front of me. It's really dirty. "I hate not knowing what's happening or who's trying to hurt me. I hate that you two think you have to watch out for me, that I'm too stupid to look after myself."

"Avery," Mel laughs my name, "you're standing on the wrong side of the railing to ask questions like that."

Sean's eyes are on me, but he doesn't move or speak. He doesn't scold Mel or hold out his hand, but I feel his gaze on the side of my face and feel the worry in his eyes.

"A fall from this height would break my leg or an ankle. Don't get me wrong, because that would suck," I say, and come back onto their side of the rail. Sitting on top of the thing, I add, "I can take care of myself most days."

"Lately, that hasn't been happening, sweetie." Mel replies. When I don't get off the banister, she flaps her arms and squeals like she can't stand it. "Get off the railing! You're freaking me out! Get down! Get down! Get down!" The tirade is enough to make Sean glance at her. Mel sucks in a deep breath of air like she's trying not to cry.

Something stirs in my stomach and I know she's reacting to something from her past. Someone did something to her and she can't bear to watch me like this now. I slip off and walk over to her, giving her a hug. "I'm sorry, Mel. I didn't mean to freak you out." Releasing her, I step back.

Mel's tough girl act flies back up as she swipes at her eyes. "Fine. Whatever."

Sean finally says, "Why don't you come with us?"

But Mel shakes her head. "Nah, I have work to do, and I need to get a new dress for this weekend. Just keep her safe." Mel turns abruptly and runs back up the stairs.

Sean presses his lips together and looks over at me. There's a question in his eyes, but I can't tell what he wants to know. "So," he says, and takes my hand. We start to walk down the stairs again. "I would have thought you were a middle child, throwing a fit like that."

"It wasn't a fit."

He smiles at me, but doesn't argue. When we push through the doors that led outside, he asks, "So, how long?" The shiny bike is parked at the back of the lot. The air is crisp and sunlight on my skin feels good. I wish it were summer and I could spend the entire day at the beach doing nothing. Technically, I guess that's two wishes. I can't remember the last time I did nothing.

"How long, what?"

A tight grin spreads across Sean's face, like he's trying to hide his judgment. He swallows hard and glances over at me from the corners of his eyes. "How long were you two together?"

My brows scrunch together. "The thought of me and Naked Guy together is barfworthy."

"Not him. Her." He jabs his thumb back to the dorm. Toward Mel.

I turn to face him with my jaw dragging on the asphalt. For a moment there are no words. His crystal blue eyes meet mine and seem worried, like I've loved someone else all this time, and not him. My chin flops around like I have no jaw bone. "We weren't together." I might as well be spitting, because I stutter so much.

He seems surprised. "Really? Like, not at all? Because I didn't see it until just now, but she cares about you a lot."

"As a friend!"

Sean shakes his head and looks back at the dorm. "To you, maybe. It's more to her, a lot more."

"You're insane."

"Like I was insane with Marty?" Sean stops in front of his bike, unfastens his helmet, and hands me mine.

"That's not the same."

"It's totally the same."

I don't know what I think about that. I glance back at the dorm and wonder if he's right. "Mel has never ever given me the vibe that she's into girls."

Sean throws his leg over the bike and starts it. "Maybe she's just into you." He smirks at me and adds, "A lot of us are. I could make a list, and I hardly know any of the people you come into contact with each day. You're addicting. Nonstop sex appeal."

My eyes hit the ground with the compliments. They knock me off kilter since he hasn't been acting that way around me. Looking up slightly, I say, "I thought there wasn't going to be any more sexy talk, Mr. Ferro."

"I never said that, Miss Stanz."

"You said you didn't want me." I nearly choke on the words. They form a knot in my throat that strangles me even after I managed to say them. I can't look at him, even though I want to. I don't want to care about him, but I do. I'm still wearing the engagement ring I bought him around my neck. I couldn't take it off. I swallow hard and feel Sean's hands wrap around mine and pull me toward him. My eyes are downcast, examining his jean-clad leg and those sexy thighs.

"I said that I didn't want to fuck you, which is very different." For a moment, neither of us speak. Sean's warm fingers feel good on my cool skin. I watch his hands, and notice how they fit over mine, like he was made for me. Ah, the musings of a crazy girl. I don't think Sean Ferro was forged for anyone. "Ask me why."

His voice is so soft, so careful, that it makes me look up. Our eyes lock and my stomach dips. "Because you don't want to buy me anymore."

"No." He smiles. "Ask me."

Parting my lips, I try to ask, but I can't. What if it's something horrible? All he's wanted of me since day one was fucking. Sex isn't an expression of love for him, so it can't be that. However, since that's the one thing I want most, I can't stand the thought of hearing something else. I'm so damaged, so incredibly messed up, that I'd rather live in my head, so I close my mouth and shake my head.

"No?" He tips his head to the side and tries to catch my gaze. "You won't ask me?"

Shaking my head again, I whisper, "Don't say things like that to me. You know how stuff is, Sean. You can't—" I break off and look him in the eye. "I know you, that's all. You don't have to say things for my benefit."

"You think I'm pretending?" He sounds surprised, but the way he looks at me says something else—like he thinks I'm a battered kitten. "I told you that I love you. I asked you to be with me. I've never said either of those things to anyone, not since before Amanda…"

That should make me happy, but it doesn't. Instead, it fills me with despair. Sean deserves happiness and he won't find it with me. Maybe we're just sucking each other down. Maybe Mel was right and two crash and burns can't save each other. Maybe Sean is just another person to talk to on the way down.

"Can you... do something for me?" I choke on my words, partly because I don't want to ask him, and partly because I wanted him to offer it.

"Anything."

I don't want to ask, but I have to. "Can you buy me for a few days? I mean, since you're here and Miss Black isn't going to like you being around me without paying. Plus, she was pissed when I lost you. And Naked Guy said he booked me this weekend. I'd rather not experience that." My lip curls in disgust that's impossible to hide. Plus, I'm pretty sure he'll hammer my ass into the ground.

Sean's face is all sympathy, right up until I mention Naked Guy. In a flash, all his emotion disappears. He pulls out his phone. Miss Black is on speed dial. Can I pick 'em or what? You never know when you'll need a hooker in a flash. I'm an ass. Besides, who am I to judge. I'm the girl who's the hooker, after all.

Biting my lip, I glance at my boots while he calls. I hear someone pick up and Sean answers, "Yes, as a matter of fact, I do. Same arrangements as last time. Yes, the same girl. Actually," he pauses and looks over at me,

"Send me two. Yes, preferably the one you sent me before with the dark skin and sharp tongue. Yes, exactly. I want them both. Is that a problem? Good." There's a pause and Sean looks down at his watch. "Nine works fine. That cost more than each of them separately." He's silent for a moment and shakes his head. "Fine, but lock in that rate for the next three weeks. It turns out that I'm not leaving town for a while. Yes...Done."

Smiling too wide for words, I jump at Sean and hug him hard. "You bought me and my besty? You're not hoping we make out in front of you, are you?" I tease.

"No. Jeeze, I try to give you guys a night off and—"

I squeal way too loud, "Awh! You're such a good man!"

Sean laughs as I crush his ribs. "Only you would be glad that I bought two call girls." The smile on his face is deep and reveals the little dimple on his cheek that I love so much.

I squee and jump on the back of Sean's bike, clutching him tightly with my thighs, as he revs the engine and takes off still laughing.

CHAPTER 10

Sean drives down to Ocean Parkway to Jones Beach, where we spend a good chunk of the afternoon. It's as close to my wish as I can get. Laying with my back in the sand, I watch the waves pound into the shore. It looks different than it did before Hurricane Sandy. The place has a different vibe, like underneath the new layers of sand and dune grass, it's still devastated—or maybe it's me who feels that way. Every day feels like a balancing act between trying to keep my feet in reality and pretending away my troubles. Too much reality all at once is a bad thing and I've already had too many bad things to last a lifetime.

I shivered a few moments ago and Sean got up without saying a word. I watched his broad back in that tight black tee shirt, and those jeans that hugs his hips perfectly, as he walked over to the store and disappeared inside. A moment later he returned with an oversized blanket and steaming cups of something good.

I sit with my arms wrapped around my ankles and let him drape the blanket over my shoulders.

He asks, "Hot chocolate or coffee?"

"Ooh, cocoa please." Sean hands it to me and sits down so we're hip to hip. I've taken off my boots, but Sean is still wearing his. I bump his shoulder gently. "There should be a NO BOOTS ON THE BEACH sign."

Sean glances down at his shoes after taking a sip of his coffee. "I'm glad there's not."

"Why would you possibly say something so hideous?" I smirk at him over the top of my cup and try to take a sip. The steam travels up my lip and warms my nose.

Sean looks at his boots and then over at me. "I didn't want to tell you this, Avery, but—I hate the feeling of the sand between my toes."

My eyes go wide and I spew the cocoa in my mouth, coughing. "No! You can't mean that!" I think back to the other times we were at the beach and he never said anything. I'm questioning everything based on this statement, like it's a pivotal point in our relationship, when Sean starts laughing.

When I turn to face him, he says, "I'm kidding. I'm just too lazy to take off my boots."

Narrowing my eyes, I give him an evil look, before glancing back at my hot cocoa. I really, really want to keep it, but there's no way I can resist. Placing the cup down in the sand, I stand and brush myself off, like he offended me. "We can't be friends anymore, Mr. Ferro. I don't joke about the beach."

Sean can tell that I'm not serious, but he doesn't react, which works fine for me when I turn and lunge at his boots. Grabbing hold of one, I wrap my arms around and pull. Sean flips backwards and makes a surprised sound as I yank harder. Well, fuck. They're stuck. He's wearing real biker boots so they're stiff as hell and they won't slip over his ankle.

THE ARRANGEMENT VOL. 10

There's an expression that I've heard but never really understood until that second: If you've got a tiger by the tail, don't let go. Catching a glimpse of Sean's eyes, I see what level of screwed I am, and it's well into orange or DEFCON 1, depending on how you look at it. DEFCON sounds more badass than colors. I like to say it out loud when no one's around. The government probably tapped my phone and assigned me my own agent because I say DEFCON way too much. If I ever get a dog, guess what his name will be? DEFCON the badass Dog!

Okay, back to the present where I'm tugging Sean's leg, literally. I could let go and expect mild retribution, or I can keep tugging and drag his butt into the surf. A wicked smile slips across my face as I pull his ankle fast and hard. Sean just managed to sit up when I start to run with his leg in my hands. He yelps and falls back into the sand again as I drag him as quickly as I can toward the water.

My problem is follow through. I have plenty of determination, so that's not what stops me. It's that I get too excited. Giggles take hold of me when I see his face. Sean realizes what I'm doing and looks like a cartoon character, which is so wrong on him, that I can't stop laughing.

Sean's lips twist into a smile a second later, "You're dead, Stanz."

"Yeah, well, you'll have to manage to get up first, Ferro." Digging my heels into the sand, I tug faster. The sand is damp and cold under my feet. We're nearly there. Sean digs his fingers into the beach, like that'll stop me.

"If you get me wet—"

I laugh and spurt out, "Psh. Like I'm ever dry around you?" A wild grin crosses my face as my cheeks burn.

Sean blinks at me and stops struggling. "You did not just say that."

Ha! A sexy diversion! Just what I needed. I keep tugging and can feel the cold water under the sand now. The waves are crashing right behind me. My plan is to pull him into a wave and then run like hell in the other direction. Good plan, right?

"I think I did," I giggle. The damn giggles tickle me so much that my body is shaking.

Sean stares at me, not realizing that the next wave will crash into us. The beach is damp and it's getting harder to pull him. Just a little bit more. I strain, but the sand has collected around his perfect butt, so now I have to pull him over a hill.

Sean flinches, like he just realized he's going to get soaked. His blue eyes go wide when he sees the massive wave coming. Close enough. Dropping his foot, I try to take off and run the other way back toward dry land, but Sean manages to whirl around and grab my ankle. I fall face first into the sand and Sean's hands grab my ankles, then my calves, and finally my hips. He rolls me over so that I'm on top of him.

Just as the wave is about to wash over us, he grins like a little boy, and says, "I should have taken off my boots, huh?"

The beach has two types of water, and it's based on the season. You can have the pleasure of swimming in damn cold water, or in the wintery wonder that's called holy-fuck-are-you-insane iceberg cold water. You can tell which one it is by the expletives coming from people's mouths when they wade in. We didn't get that chance, but it was the latter. Squared. With a penguin on top. Holy fuck.

The wave washes over us, swallowing Sean and I whole. He doesn't release me, but I can feel the ocean pulling us back as the wave recedes. Sand rushes by my hands as I try to pull away. Somehow, Sean manages to sit up and hold me in his arms. Seaweed is tangled in my hair and touching my face, and my underpants are mostly sand at this point.

I'm shivering and yelling, but Sean just laughs. "You're such an ass!" I beat my fists into his chest and try to get up. Another wave is about to break. Sean's fingers are locked around my waist.

When I look up at him, his eyes glitter with mischief, and he shakes his head. "And it's a lovely ass too, or so I hear." He grins at me. "Get ready for round two."

"You wouldn't."

"I would." His arms lock around my waist as icy cold water crashes into my back. Screaming, I hold onto him and cling.

When the water rushes back into the ocean I start laughing again. My hair is dripping ice cubes down my back. I shiver and look at him. Sean rarely looks this happy. It's like every worry, every pain he's ever had, was washed away. It makes me want to stay here with him, which is complete crazy talk because it's freezing. "I think there are icicles in my panties."

"Don't talk about your panties unless you want me to rip them off."

I giggle way too much. After I manage to put on a straight face, I lower my voice and speak seriously. "Mr. Ferro."

"Miss Stanz." His eyes lock on mine, but the corners of his mouth twitch like he's repressing a grin.

"When did we get so formal?"

"We didn't," he says casually. "You only call me by my proper name when you're aroused."

My face scrunches as my jaw drops. I'm ready to contest it, to deny his accusation to the death, but a wave hits my back and I shriek as I fall into him. I had no idea my voice could hit that note, or that Sean could laugh so much. His warm hands hold me in place on his lap as the sand around us washes back into the ocean with the wave. His hips are half buried.

My shirt is frozen and stuck to my body. When I breathe it feels like I'm trying to suck in snow cones, but I gasp because Sean takes my breath away. He always has. My eyes drift to his mouth, to those perfect lips and that beautiful smile. For a second, it feels real. I'm not his hooker. I'm not his friend. I'm not his lover, but I want to be. I want to be anything and everything, so I lean in before he stops smiling and press my mouth to his. The heat, the warmth of his lips, stands in strong contrast to the cold water. When I feel his smile fade, I pull back and watch his eyes. I don't know what I'm looking for, but it feels like I should find it there.

However, his gaze is lower. At first I think he's looking at my chest. He could get a puncture wound, my nipples are so hard. Why does it feel like I crossed a line? Disappointment floods through me until I realize he's looking at the ring around my neck. It's under my shirt, plastered to my chest. Another wave washes over us, but Sean manages to pull the ring out before the water rushes away.

"You're still wearing it?" He sounds shocked and blinks a few times like the piece of jewelry will disappear if he looks away.

I shrug, like it doesn't mean anything. "Just around you."

"You're always around me." Sean looks up slowly, his face expressionless.

"Then, I'll wear it for a while," I laugh uneasily and press my finger to his nose like he's a little kid. "Can't have you forgetting what you missed out on."

"No, we wouldn't want that." His eyes shift down and he looks side to side, scanning the beach. I don't know what he means, if he's teasing me or if he's being serious.

Either way, I don't want to ruin whatever just happened. After everything that's gone down, I needed this so badly and Sean seemed to know. I push off his lap and hold out my hand for him. My clothes stick to my body and I shiver as the wind hits me. It leaves very little to the imagination when clothing looks like skin.

Sean takes my hand and manages to get up before the next wave crashes. He pulls me against him and whispers in my ear, "We should do something to get warm."

I press my lips together, still smiling so hard that my face hurts. "Ah, my call girl services don't start until seven."

"No, my dear," Sean leans in and whispers in my ear. "I'm afraid you misunderstood. I'll be servicing you."

Giggling, I snap my fingers. "Sweatpants and hot cocoa?" He nods and rubs his hands up my back, pulling me against him. "Hot soup and fresh bread? Oooh! Lobster Soup?" I nearly have an orgasm thinking about it. I'm so cold and the thought alone of anything that warm is stimulating me in all the right ways. Mmmm. Soup.

Sean gives me a crooked smirk, revealing that dimple again. "Anything you want. Anything at all." He winks and I chortle.

"I might want more than soup." Maybe. Taking off my clothes sounds like suckage at the moment, but I think being naked must be better. I'm an Avery-sicle complete with chattering teeth.

Sean laughs and holds me tight. He lifts my feet off the ground, spinning me in a circle. When he puts me down, he presses his forehead to mine and says, "I was hoping you'd say that."

CHAPTER 11

Sean buys a truck load of JONES BEACH crap from the vendor since neither of us brought a change of clothes, and soon we're walking down the new boardwalk, hand in hand.

"Where are we going? I was promised soup, Ferro. Don't screw with me. I'm still frozen."

Sean makes a noise in the back of his throat that sounds an awful lot like humming before he glances over at me. "In good time, short one."

"Short one? Are you Yoda now? Sensei? Or what? Besides, I prefer vertically challenged...and a cup of soup." I stomp my flip flops and fold my arms over my chest.

Sean stops and smiles at me, snaking his fingers under the hem of my huge ass sweatshirt as he looks down at me. "You are such a baby when you're hungry."

My bottom lip juts out and I'm whining, "I am not," before I can stop myself. A million excuses fill my head, but I realize that I don't need to say any of them. Sean's not complaining. In fact, he seems to like it.

Huh, turns out my mom was wrong. Whining isn't unattractive. I wish she was here to have that discussion. My thoughts drift a little more before I look up at him again. It's unreal how many different thoughts can fly through my mind at once. I'm not a logical person. My mind is a vortex, always swirling like a twister, ripping apart everything I'm seeing and hearing and trying to make sense of it. Like the man standing in front of me. This is a softer version of Sean. I've seen this edition a few times and I know he won't stay like this for long. It's something about this place, or that he's intentionally unguarded right now. Or maybe it's because he got wet and I fed him after midnight. I have no idea what made him act like this today, but I wish I saw more of this side of him. Sean seems to keep it locked away, like this side of his personality doesn't exist. Maybe that's what he wants people to think, because this part of him is clearly vulnerable. Even I can see that.

He slips his hand under my shirt and says, "What if I told you that I had dinner all arranged, but I forgot the soup?"

The corners of my mouth tip down as I consider his statement. "No soup?"

"I seriously doubt it. As it is, I gave the chef a coronary telling him to make dinner so fast. I almost suggested hamburgers, but I think he would have fired me." Sean kisses my cheek and then takes my hand, pulling me toward one of the closed buildings. I assume that we'll walk under the portico and out to the parking lot on the other side, but he stops and pulls the door open for me.

"Are we looting a state park gift shop?" I joke, and look over my shoulder at him. "Ooh! Dibs on the park passes! I'm going to cover myself in Empire Passport stickers!" There's a huge smile on my face. I probably look like a deranged circus clown.

"What are you talking about?"

"The parking pass thingie that sticks on the car window so you get into the park for free. You don't get out much, do you?"

Sean holds the door as I stand there, looking up at him. "I seriously wonder about you. It's like there's an old lady and a toddler fighting for control of your brain."

I flick his nose and laugh. "The old lady won tonight, sonny. She's a little crotchety since she's learned that she's not getting any soup!"

Smiling, he says, "Go inside, lunatic."

"Make me, Mr. Ferro." I say it lightly, teasingly. I don't think Sean will do anything. He never does, so when he leans in close, his face a breath from mine, and makes a purring sound in the back of his throat, my jaw drops. As soon as he stops, I want to hear it again. I can't remember why we're standing in a doorway or what we were talking about. That sound is rarer than that dimple, which been begging to be licked all day. Do you know how hard it is NOT to lick Sean Ferro? Add that dimple and I'm lost. But the deep, husky sound that came from Sean, from my

Sean—oh my God—kill me now. I could die happy.

"Aroused again, Miss Stanz?"

Pressing my lips together, I stop gaping and punch his side. "Jerk."

He laughs. "Translation: hells yeah." I look over my shoulder as we walk over the threshold, and wonder if I know him at all. Since I keep wondering that, I assume that I don't. When you know a person, they stop surprising you, don't they? If he does anything else I might die of shock. Ooops. Spoke too soon.

My feet suddenly stop as my mouth falls open. "What did you do?" The little shop has been cleared out so that there's only a single dining table, complete with drippy candles, and two chairs. White twinkle lights surround the room, hidden in pale flowy fabric that mimics the waves. The sound and scent of the ocean fills my head, but the fireplace next to the table warms the room. The scents of fall, sea water, and crackling wood mix together.

"I thought you might need a nice night." Sean sounds uncertain, like he isn't sure if I like it.

Turning slowly, I look up at him. "You did this for me?" He nods. "When?" Other than the altercation with Naked Guy, Sean has been with me all day. I can't imagine when he had time to arrange it.

Looking at me through those thick, dark lashes, he says, "When we first got here. You ran into the ladies room, and I called my mother's chef and had him come out along with a few of her designers to make the room a little better. I just had to keep you from freezing to death before now. I didn't plan on going for a swim."

"You should have taken off your boots." I grin at him.

Sean steps toward me, his eyes darkening, and that sexy smile on his lips. He brushes the back of his hand along my cheek before whispering in my ear. "I'm glad I didn't." I shiver, but it has nothing to do with being cold.

CHAPTER 12

Course after course is brought out to the table on silver trays. Beautiful Ferro china plates that cost more than my car are placed in front of me with little portions of food. I stare at my main course without moving to pick up a fork. My head is tilted to the side slightly as I look at my plate.

"What's wrong?" Sean ask. "I thought you liked chicken cordon bleu, and those little carrots."

My bottom lip quivers and I can see the horror spreading across Sean's face like spilled paint. I rush to wipe away the look before I ruin all his hard work. I would have never thought he'd do something like this for me, ever. Reaching across the table, I take his hand and pat it. "I do. I mean, I haven't had a meal like this since my parents died. The only time I eat chicken cordon bleu is at Wendy's. And I do love little carrots. This is beyond words, Sean."

My stomach sinks as my old life clashes with the new one. This man is trying so hard to make me smile, but he conjured ghosts with his gift. When I look up at him, I try my best to blind him with a bright smile, but he sees the sadness in my eyes. I'm such a train wreck. Sniffling, I smile and ask, "Who cries over cute little carrots?" My vision blurs as my eyes brim with tears.

Without a word, Sean stands, walks over to my seat, and holds out his hand. The chef comes out, looking rather horrified, and covers the plates with silvery domes before disappearing into the back room again. Seeing Sean's hard body in a soft sweat suit is so strange. My eyes travel over him once more before I take his hand and apologize.

Sean pulls me into his arms and holds me for a moment. Then music starts playing. It's a slow song, something that I haven't heard in a long time. Sean takes my hand as he steps back and pulls me with him. His other hand drops to my waist. Looking down at me, he slides his flip flopped feet across the floor and I can't help but smile. "You can dance?"

"And you can follow. Who knew?" he teases, as he grips my hand loosely and leads me under his arm so I do a slow spin before coming back to him.

"I can follow." He laughs. "Okay, that's a lie. I can follow sometimes, when my mood is right."

"And the waning moon is hung in the winter sky, just to the right of Jupiter—" Sean makes an *oof* sound as I elbow him.

"Didn't your mother teach you manners? You seem to say whatever snide remark is floating through your mind." The memories of my mother's voice and wintery nights in our warm little house are no longer strangling me now that I'm in his arms.

How am I supposed to reconcile my past with my present? It seems impossible. People told me that one day the memories won't hurt so much, but each time one pops up, it feels like I've been hit over the head with a shovel. One day I'll smile and the grief won't be there. Such thoughts seem like fairy tales. I'm more likely to find an alligator wearing a tutu on the subway, than think of my parents and smile without feeling any pain.

Sean's voice tightens. "My mother taught me many things. She's a ruthless, cold woman, and not the person who you'd want me to emulate."

"Oh." Before I manage to completely mess up the evening, I add, "Then tell me, if you could pattern yourself after someone, who would it be?"

He smiles and the coldness in his eyes melts. "You."

I think he's joking, but he stops dancing and takes both my hands in his. "I'm serious. You're warm and kind. You don't hide who you are or what you think. You wear your heart on your sleeve even though it's been fractured. When you care for someone, you do it wholly and not in part. You don't hold back. You're not selfish. Not once have you asked me for anything, even though you need everything. You're borderline destitute and you haven't asked me for a dime."

Sean's lashes lower as he speaks and he continues the slow dance that's turned into more of a rocking hug. His voice sounds strained, like these things are difficult to say. "You're lonely and I'm alone. It seemed like a good fit, like we complement each other, but it's more than that. You saw it and I didn't. When you said you were going to propose to me, every part of me protested to the idea. Marriage is something that nearly destroyed me before, but since I met you—I don't know."

Sean looks down at the floor before glancing up at me with those gem colored eyes. "When you said you wouldn't ask me to marry you, I didn't like it. It made me think of the little house and wonder what it would be like to live there with you—to hear your voice echoing through the halls every day. It made me wonder what I could do that would make you think I was worth marrying."

"And what'd you come up with?" My head is floating off my shoulders. There's nothing he could have said that would have made me light up more.

Taking a deep breath, Sean replies, "Nothing. There is nothing I can do to make me deserve someone like you. No matter how hard I try, no matter what I do, you'll always be a better person than I am, which is why I can't let you go."

His words make my stomach flip and I stop breathing. We stop moving. I had been thinking that he's just talking, saying things I want to hear, until he said that part. "What do you mean?"

Sean smiles and tucks a stray hair behind my ear. "I mean exactly that. I can't let you go. I'll take you any way I can get you. If I have to buy you from Black, I will. If I have to share you," his jaw tightens but he manages to say it, "because you want to keep working for her, I will. I will do and be anything you want, as long as I can be near you. Avery, you make me a better man. Without you, well, there's nothing. I'm lost in darkness and you're my only ray of light." Sean lowers himself so he's on one knee and looks up at me.

The smile I'm wearing falls off and thuds on the floor. What is he doing? I stagger back as he kneels in front of me. My heart slams into my ribs and falls over. This can't be happening. I'm dreaming, or I'm dead. Is he proposing? He can't be? But he's kneeling. A cold chill works its way through my body, tickling my insides, as it passes through my chest and settles in my stomach. My throat tightens as I lock my jaw to keep from speaking. I blink rapidly, trying not to rip my hand away, because I fear this is some cruel joke, but Sean's not laughing. Not at all.

He's reaching into his pocket and pulls something out. Lifting it up to me, I can see the perfect little circle with a bright diamond on top. There are two side stones, each one a sapphire as blue as his eyes. Pressing my lips together, I stare at the ring and try to blink the stinging sensation out of my eyes.

Looking up at me, Sean continues, "I wish I were more eloquent, that I had a better way with words, but I'm afraid I'm utterly lacking. There's no profession that will convince you. There's no testament of adoration to persuade you. I'm afraid that this is all there is and all I have to offer. I'm a broken man that you brought back from the abyss. I know I don't deserve you, and it's selfish for me to ask, but I have to. You've lit up my life too brightly, for too long, and made it so I can't tolerate the shadows anymore. So, I must ask you a question."

The moment is so unreal that I don't realize I've spoken until I hear my voice. "Ask me…"

TURN THE PAGE TO READ A
FREE SAMPLE OF:

STRIPPED

A FERRO FAMILY NOVEL

CHAPTER 1

CASSIE

Bruce claps his big beefy hands at us like we're misbehaving dogs. "Come on ladies! Hustle! The bachelor party isn't going to be much fun if we never get there. Damn, Gretchen, you aren't even dressed, yet?"

She laughs like he's funny, even though Bruce is as far from funny as a person could get. He's the bouncer at the club and on nights like tonight, he comes with us to keep the guys from getting handsy. Some rich brat out on Long Island rented us for the night. There are seven of us going to perform on stage, plus the stripping wait staff, and dear, sweet, Bruce.

Gretchen is piling her long golden hair onto the top of her head and securing it with a long bobby pin. She's strutting around half naked, as if we like looking at her. She smiles sweetly at Bruce and waves a hand, bending it at the wrist like he's silly. "Please, I'll be ready before Cassie even finishes lacing up her corset."

She tilts her head in my direction as I fumble with my corset hooks. Every time I manage to hook one, another comes undone. Whoever invented the corset should be burned at the stake. The stupid thing might look cool once it's on, but getting into it is a whole other matter. Add in the fact that mine is a real corset—meaning it has steel boning—and breathing isn't something I can do either. I got this thing because it was authentic. I thought that meant it had period fabric or grommets or something cool. It turns out that authentic means metal rods built into the bodice, guaranteed to bruise my ribs. Fuck, I hate this thing, but I refuse to throw it away—it cost me three weeks' pay at my old job. Plus, it's not like I wear it every night. We only pull out the good stuff on holidays and for special events like this.

Bruce turns his head my way and looks like he wants to pull out his hair. I'm nearly dressed, except for this contraption. My ensemble includes the candy apple colored corset, lace-topped thigh highs, and a delicate little G-string, coupled with heels that could be used as weapons. If I ever get mugged wearing these shoes, you can bet your ass that I won't run, not that I could. These are the things I think about when I make my purchases. Can this purse do some damage? Maybe I should skip the leather Dooney and grab me that metal no-name bag with the sharp corners. My roommate and I live across the street from a drug den. Don't even get me started on that. I know we need to move, but knowing it and affording it are two different things. In the meantime, I buy accessories that can be used as weapons.

Glaring at her, I reply, "Gee, thanks, Gretch." My fingers push the next bit of metal through the grommet. This one stays put.

She bats her glittering lashes at me. "No problem." Gretchen is tall and lanky with a larger-than-life super model thing going on. I hate her. She's a bitch with a capital B. It's all good, though. She hates me, too. It's difficult to be hostile toward someone that likes you. Gretchen makes it easy to hate her guts.

Me, I'm not a supermodel. I'm nothing to look at—my mom drilled that into my head a million times. I'm completely average with sub-par confidence, but I can act. I can fake it so that once I hit that stage, I'm as good as the rest of the strippers.

No, I didn't dream of being a pole dancer when I was a little kid, but my life took some wicked turns and here I am, dealing with it. There are worse things I suppose, although I won't be able to think of a single one when I'm letting a bunch of pervs rake their lusty eyes over my naked body. The truth is, I hate this. I'd rather be anywhere else, doing anything else. The gynecologist's office, sign me up. Root canal, no problem. I'll be there early and with a smile on my face. Anything is better than this.

Bruce lingers in the dressing room for too long, staring at his watch. His thick arms are folded over his broad chest as he watches the second hand tick off the passing time. He ignores Gretch's gibe at me. I may be newer, but I pull in a lot more cash and that's what the boss likes—lots of money. As long as I keep doing it, I have a job.

I finally get my corset hooked up when Beth walks by. She's already wearing some frilly satin thing. "Hey, Cassie. Do you want me to lace you up?"

Tucking a piece of hair behind my ear, I nod. "Yeah, thanks." She laces me in, pulling each X tightly, cinching me up until I can barely breathe. "Tight enough?"

I try to inhale deeply, and can't because the metal bars inside the fabric won't permit it. I nod and press my hands to the bodice, feeling the supple satin under my hands. "Yeah, tighter than that and I'll pass out—or pop a boob."

She laughs, "You're the only one who worries about stuff like that. You're so cute." She ties off the strings and tucks them in before swatting my back when she's finished. My boobs are hiked up so high that I can't see my toes when I look down. I grab my robe and wrap it around me as we head to the cars. It's going to be a long night.

———

The ride to the party is short. We're on the north shore of Long Island, not too far from the coast. There are tons of old homes with huge lawns and even bigger estate houses nestled out of sight between towering oaks and pines. The place hosting the party looks like a castle. We pass through the gates and drive around to the side of the house. The van stops and we're told the usual—go wait in the servants' wing until it's time.

Beth and I walk inside, shoulder to shoulder, whispering about the garish wealth that's practically dripping from the walls as we walk inside. Gretchen and a few other girls trail behind us, chattering about what kind of tips they'll make tonight. A party like this can line a girl's pockets for a month if it goes well, but for me it'll do more than that. You see, I'm the main event, the mystery girl in the pink room—the bachelor's private-party dancer. While my coworkers are off in the main hall, I'll be earning the big bucks. That's the main reason why Gretchen hates my guts. Before I came along, she was the top stripper around here.

It's getting late, which means the party is well under way. Beth picks up a tiny sandwich off a tray as she walks to the back of the bustling room. "You think this guy knows what's coming?"

I shrug. "Like it matters, anyway? When's the last time we were sent away?"

"Uh, never." She pops the food in her mouth and chews it up.

I'm leaning against a counter top with my elbows behind me, supporting my weight. "My point exactly. Guys are dicks. They commit to marrying a woman, but this kind of crap the night before the wedding is okay." I roll my eyes as I make a disgusted sound, and straighten up. All of a sudden I'm talking with my hands and they're flying all over the place, "Tell me, why would a guy want a lap dance if he's in love? You'd think he'd only want his bride, but that never happens. He's always happy to have an ass in his face."

"Well, your ass is pretty awesome, or so I've heard." Beth smirks at me and glances around the kitchen. We're in the way, but there isn't anywhere else for us to go yet.

"Guys suck, that's all I'm saying."

"I know. You've said it a million times." She makes a *roaring* sound and shakes her fist in the air before turning to me and grunting, "Men. Evil."

"You're an idiot." I smile at her, trying not to laugh.

She points at me and clicks her tongue. "Right back at you, Cassie."

Bruce waves us over to the other side of the kitchen. "Cassie, Beth—follow me." We duck out behind him and follow the guy down the hall and slip into a little room. It's been done up in pale pinks with silver curtains, similar to the room I work in at the club. Since this is a party, Bruce added another dancer and I got to choose. While I work the stage at the front of the room, Beth will work the floor.

Bruce points a beefy finger at the stage and says to us, "Take your places, and remember that this client is the shit. Pull out all the stops, say 'no' to nothing. You got it?"

We nod in unison. The stage is elevated off the floor, with a few steps up at either end. It looks like the stage is new, built just for me. People usually rent those gray, make-shift stages that wobble when walked on, but not this guy. They spared no expense. The walls are lined with pale pink silks and illuminated from the floor. Clear tables flicker around the room with pink flames dancing within. It's seductive. The colors blend together, reminding me of pale flesh and kissable pink lips. As I climb the steps up the side of the stage and head to the silvery tinsel curtain, I call back to Beth. "Who is this party for again? And why is he the shit? I must have missed the memo."

She laughs as she's examining one of the lights within the glass table. It looks like fire, but it can't be since it's pink. She looks up at me. "Dr. Peter Granz, and he's the shit because he's a Ferro. Hence the swank party." Beth looks up when I don't answer.

I rush at Beth, nearly knocking her over. My jaw is hanging open as worry darts across my face faster than I can contain it. "Ferro?"

"Yeah, why?"

I'm in melt down mode. "I can't be here." I glance around the room and look at the door longingly. Before I make up my mind to run, I hear male voices approaching. Fuck! My heart pounds faster in my chest. If he's here, if Jonathan sees me—the thought cuts off before it finishes.

I'm ready to bounce out the window when Beth grabs my wrist and hauls me to the front of the room. She shoves me behind the curtain and hisses in my ear, "If you freak out now, Gretchen will steal your job. Snap out of it. Whoever this guy is, he isn't worth it."

The tinsel curtain in front of me flutters, but it conceals both of us for the moment. The male voices grow louder until the door is yanked open. The curtain rustles and I'm in full freak-out mode. He can't be here. He can't see me like this. At the same time, Beth's right. I can't skip out. Bruce will run me over with the van and there's no way in hell they'll ever give me another cent.

I stand there, frozen, unable to think. Every muscle in my body is strained, ready to run, but I don't move. My bare feet remain glued to the floor as I smash my lips together.

Then, I hear it—that voice. It floats through the air like a familiar old song. Oh God, someone shoot me. I can't do this. "You don't know what you're talking about. What guy wouldn't want a party like this?" Jonathan is talking to someone in that light, charming, tone of his.

"Uh, your brother, Peter. Do you know the guy at all? He's going to act like he loves it and get the hell out before you can blink." Glancing through the curtains, I can see the second man. He has dark hair and bright blue eyes like Jonathan. The only difference is their posture. Jonathan has all his weight thrown onto one hip with his arms folded across his chest. The other guy's spine is ramrod straight, like he's never slouched in his life.

Peering at Jonathan through the tinsel, I see a perfect smile lace his lips. "Sean, I know him better than that. Pete is going to love this. It's exactly the kind of party I'd want if I was getting hitched."

"Yes, I know." Sean's voice is flat. He glances around the room with disgust, and slips his hands into his pockets. "Don't say I didn't warn you."

"Oh come on! It's Peter. What's he going to do?"

Sean laughs, like he knows something that Jonathan doesn't. "Don't let that English teacher façade fool you, Jonny. He's as hot headed as I am. No one fucks with him. He's going to consider this a slap in the face, an insult to Sidney. Cancel the strippers before he gets here." Sean leaves the room without another word.

Jonathan Ferro lets out a rush of air and runs his fingers through his thick, dark, hair. The aggravated sound that comes out of his mouth kills me. I've heard it before, I know him too well to not be affected by it. That's the sound he makes when he knows he's screwed up, when he sees that he isn't the man he wants to be. There's always been this wall between Jonathan and his family. I guess he still hasn't gotten past it. Jon paces in a circle a few times and then darts out of the room.

"Holy shit." Beth looks at me and hisses, "What happened between you and him?"

It feels like icy fingers have wrapped around my heart and squeezed. I stare after him and utter, "Nothing, absolutely nothing."

STRIPPED IS ON SALE NOW

"Sexy, funny, intense, excruciatingly exquisite..."

"The Ferro Legacy lives and never disappoints! Suspense, romance and a non-stop page turner."

"Jonathan just might be my favorite."

MORE FERRO FAMILY BOOKS

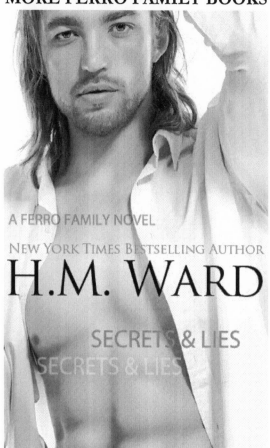

A FERRO FAMILY NOVEL

NEW YORK TIMES BESTSELLING AUTHOR

H.M. WARD

SECRETS & LIES

SECRETS & LIES

Coming Soon

BRYAN FERRO
~THE PROPOSITION~
Coming this fall

*****

SEAN FERRO
~THE ARRANGEMENT~

******

PETER FERRO GRANZ
~DAMAGED~

******

JONATHAN FERRO
~STRIPPED~

MORE ROMANCE BOOKS BY

H.M. WARD

DAMAGED (A Novel)

DAMAGED 2

STRIPPED

SCANDALOUS

SCANDALOUS 2

SECRETS

THE SECRET LIFE OF TRYSTAN
SCOTT

And more.

To see a full book list, please visit:

www.SexyAwesomeBooks.com/books.htm

CAN'T WAIT FOR

H.M WARD'S NEXT

STEAMY BOOK?

⭐⭐⭐⭐⭐

Let her know by leaving stars and telling
her what you liked about
THE ARRANGEMENT VOL. 10
in a review!

Made in the USA
Lexington, KY
09 November 2013